You can be a
Brownie Girl Scout, too!

If you are 6, 7, or 8 years old, or in the 1st, 2nd, or 3rd grade, just ask your parents to look in your local telephone directory under "Girl Scouts," and call for information. You can also ask your parents to call **Girl Scouts of the U.S.A.** at **1-(212) 852-8000** or write to 420 Fifth Avenue, New York, NY 10018-2702 to find out about becoming a Girl Scout in your area.

For all my fellow campers
in Troop 2667, Arlington, Virginia — J. O'C.

To Steve — L.S.L.

Copyright © 1993 by Girl Scouts of the United States of America. All rights reserved. Published by Grosset & Dunlap, Inc., a member of The Putnam & Grosset Group, New York, in cooperation with Girl Scouts of the United States of America. Published simultaneously in Canada. Printed in the U.S.A.

Library of Congress Cataloging-in-Publication Data

O'Connor, Jane.
    Amy's (not so) great camp-out / by Jane O'Connor ; illustrated by Laurie Struck Long.
        p.   cm. — (Here come the Brownies ; 4)
    Summary: Popular in her Brownies troop because she is always so much fun, Amy worries that she will lose her popularity when she gets sick on a camp-out and can't participate in any of the activities.
    [1. Girl Scouts—Fiction.   2. Camping—Fiction.   3. Friendship—Fiction.]
I. Long, Laurie Struck, ill.   II. Title.   III. Series.
PZ7.0222Am   1993
[Fic]—dc20   92-45881

ISBN 0-448-40166-5 (pbk.) A B C D E F G H I J

ISBN 0-448-40167-3 (GB) A B C D E F G H I J

HERE COME THE BROWNIES
A Brownie Girl Scout Book

Amy's (Not So) Great Camp-Out

By Jane O'Connor
Illustrated by Laurie Struck Long

Grosset & Dunlap • New York
In association with GIRL SCOUTS OF THE U.S.A.

1

"Amy, you're going on a camp-out. So why on earth are you packing those monster claws?" Amy's mother asked.

"You never know. They might come in handy." Amy laughed at her own joke. "Get it, Ma? Handy!" Then she threw the claws into her bag. Amy had bought them last Halloween. They were big and rubbery and fit over her hands like gloves.

Amy could just picture it. . . . Later

tonight, there she'd be, sitting around a campfire with a bunch of her Brownie friends. It would be her turn to tell a ghost story. She'd make up a really scary one. Maybe about a monster whose claws had been cut off. And he's still searching for them. . . . Or maybe about some kids on a beach who find an old chest. They think they have found buried treasure. They open the chest. They are sure they will see lots of gold and jewels. But no! All they find is a pair of . . . horrible monster claws! Amy imagined whipping out the claws in front of all her friends. She could almost hear the screams now. It was going to be so cool!

"Amy. Amy. You're not listening to me, honey."

"Sorry, Ma. I was just thinking about

how much fun this camp-out is going to be."

"Yes, I know. But I want to make sure you have everything you need." Her mother began to read from the checklist that Mrs. Q., Amy's troop leader, had sent home. "Sleeping bag...water bottle...plastic cup...jacket..." Amy's mother went down the list.

"Yes, Ma. It's all here." Amy inspected the large pile in front of them. Mrs. Q. had said to bring only what you really needed.

And only what you could pack and carry yourself. With some pushing and poking, Amy managed to squeeze everything into her duffel bag.

"And you're sure you feel well enough to go?" Amy's mother looked uncertain.

"I am fine, Ma. Fine." And she was... except for a funny little wobbly feeling in her tummy. But Amy was not going to tell her mother that. Yesterday Amy had to stay home from school because she had a tummy ache. But she did feel much better today. Really. And anyhow, there was no way Amy was missing this camp-out. Amy had been looking forward to it for weeks.

On the last camp-out it never stopped raining. Even so, Amy had had a great time. Mrs. Q. had brought along a big box full of makeup and face paints. There had been a face-painting contest. And Amy won for Craziest. She had painted her face to look like a fried egg. She still kept the picture Mrs. Q. had taken on her dresser.

"Well, just promise me you'll take it easy. You don't always have to be the life of the party, you know. The fun does not depend on you."

Amy held up her right hand. "Girl Scout's honor. I will really try to take it easy. The troop will hardly know I'm there."

Then the phone rang.

It was Amy's friend, Corrie. Corrie had moved into Amy's neighborhood a few months ago. This was Corrie's first year in Brownies. And this was her very first camp-out.

"So?" Corrie sounded nervous. "What did she say?"

"Ma says I can go!" Amy told her.

"Oh, that makes me feel so much better," Corrie said.

Amy and Corrie were going to be buddies for the camp-out. Buddies slept next to each other in the tent. Buddies were partners on hikes. Buddies were supposed to look after each other.

"You know, I've never been so far away from home before. Just think. We're going to be sleeping in a different state." The way Corrie said "state" made it sound like they were going to another planet. Corrie paused. Then she said, "I hope I don't get homesick and want to go home."

"You won't," Amy promised. "We'll be having too much fun. And look. We're buddies. I'll be right there. All the time. If you wake up in the middle of the night and feel lonely, just wake me up, too. I'll keep you company."

"Amy, you are such a great friend," Corrie said.

Then Amy's father and sister called to her, "Hurry, Amy. We're supposed to be at the pickup spot in fifteen minutes."

"Well, hi," Amy said to Corrie. "I won't see you in a long time."

Corrie giggled. That was opposite talk. It meant "Bye, I'll see you soon."

After they hung up, Amy put on her favorite baseball hat. The one with the red felt arrow through it. She picked up her sleeping bag and duffel. Yes! She could carry everything herself. Then she went through the front door.

The fun was about to begin!

2

Amy was nearly the last Brownie to arrive. Most of the other girls in her troop were already on the big yellow school bus.

"Well, look who's here!" Mrs. Q. came over and put an arm around Amy. "I heard you were sick yesterday. But you look fine today.... I'm so happy you made it."

Several heads popped out of the bus windows.

"Look! It's Amy!"

"We were so worried that you weren't coming."

"The camp-out wouldn't be half as much fun without you."

Amy grinned. Ah! This was music to her ears!

Then Amy gave her parents and sister a hug and climbed on board.

"Ooh, Amy. Sit here!" someone said.

"No, Amy. Sit with us. We can squeeze three in a seat."

"No, me! Please." Somebody tugged on Amy's arm. "I saved this seat for you."

It was Mrs. Q. who settled the seating question. She stood at the front of the bus. She held up her right hand. That was the Girl Scout sign for quiet.

All the girls held up their right hands, too.

"Now remember, Brownie Girl Scouts, everybody has a buddy on this camp-out. Buddies look out for each other. And buddies are bus partners. So, Amy, who is your buddy?"

"Corrie. But she's not here yet."

"Then find a seat and wait for her."

Amy did. A minute later Corrie made her way down the aisle and slid in next to her.

Corrie squeezed Amy's hand. "Ooh," she said. "I'm so excited...and soooo nervous!"

"I promise you. It is going to be a great time," Amy said. "The greatest time ever."

Then the bus driver beeped the horn. Mrs. Q. counted heads. Twenty-six girls. And seven grown-ups.

"Well, we're ready to roll. Everybody buckle up," Mrs. Q. called out.

They were off.

The bus ride was long...and bumpy...
and noisy. One girl had a little push-button
scream machine.

Right away some girls started singing.

"Found a peanut, found a peanut,
  Found a peanut last night,
  Last night I found a peanut,
  Found a peanut last night."

The tune went to "My Darling Clementine." There were about a million verses to the song. And Amy always liked to keep on singing until the very end. But today the song sounded so loud, like a radio turned up too high.

Then the bus hit a bump in the road. And Amy's tummy did a little flip-flop.

"Hey, Amy!" Somebody poked her in the back. Amy turned around. It was Lauren. She was sitting in the row right behind Amy.

"I really <u>hate</u> you!" Lauren said. "I am so <u>sorry</u> you came."

That was opposite talk again. What Lauren was saying was "I really like you. I am so glad you came."

Amy knew Lauren expected her to say something funny back. It was Amy who first got everybody talking in opposite talk. That was after Mrs. Fujikawa, their teacher, taught 2-B all about antonyms. But the bus bounced some more. And all Amy could think about was her tummy.

"It was rotten,

It was rotten,

It was rotten last night..."

On and on the girls sang. Amy stuck her fingers in her ears. She was sick of hearing about rotten peanuts! Ugh!

Corrie tapped Amy on the shoulder.

Amy unplugged her ears.

"Are you feeling okay?" Corrie asked.

Amy frowned. "I don't know. It's just so bumpy. And so noisy in here."

"Do you want me to tell Mrs. Q.? She'll make everybody quiet down."

"No! Please don't do that!" The last thing Amy wanted was for Mrs. Q. to make everybody be quiet because of her. She liked making things more fun. Not less. That's what everyone expected of her, too.

Corrie looked unsure. "But I'm your buddy. If you're not feeling so good, I should tell Mrs. Q."

"I am fine. Really. Just fine. And I bet we'll be there soon."

"Maybe you will feel better if you close your eyes," Corrie said. "I know. Hold out your arm. I'll tickle it for you. You always like that."

Amy held out her arm.

Corrie ran her fingers up and down Amy's arm. Most kids couldn't stand it for even ten seconds. But Amy was not ticklish at all. To her it felt nice, like little raindrops falling on her. Amy smiled and closed her eyes. She was glad that Corrie was her buddy.

It was funny how they were such good

friends. They were not at all alike. Corrie was quiet. But once you got to know her, she was very fun and interesting. Corrie was the best artist in 2-B. And she had lots of other talents, too. Corrie knew how to play

cat's cradle better than anybody. Corrie could speak Spanish. And Corrie could wiggle her ears.

Corrie's fingers were still running up and down Amy's arm. Up and down. Amy kept her eyes closed. Just for another second. They were sure to be at the campground soon.

3

The next thing Amy knew, someone was shaking her. Hard.

"Wake up! Wake up! We're here!"

It was Corrie.

"What?" Amy yawned and rubbed her eyes. Girls were already filing off the bus.

"We're here," Corrie said again.

Amy licked her lips. They felt all dry. "I can't believe I fell asleep." That was something only little kids did on bus rides.

But her tummy felt better now. "Some fun bus partner I turned out to be."

"That's okay. I'm so glad you're here," Corrie said, following Amy off the bus.

Amy took a long look around. "Yes," she said to Corrie. "It's just like I remember."

There was the lake with clear, crayon blue water. Green tents on wooden platforms

were on one side of the lake by a tall flagpole. Farther back was the main campsite. And beyond that was a two-story wooden house. It was called Blue Water Lodge. It was where everybody ate and played games if it rained. But from where they were standing, Amy couldn't see it. All she could see were trees, trees, and more trees.

"Gee! We really are out in the wild," Corrie said.

"It's not the wild, Corrie. It's just nature," Amy assured her. "Believe me, the wildest thing you will see all weekend is a chipmunk. Right, Sarah?"

Sarah nodded. "Maybe a couple of deer if we get lucky. But no bears or wolves or anything scary."

Corrie looked relieved. Sarah knew all about animals. She was going to be a veterinarian when she grew up.

"Then lead the way!" Corrie said.

Besides Sarah and Corrie, Amy was sharing a tent with Marsha, Lauren, and Jo Ann. Mrs. Q. was the grown-up who would be sleeping with them.

"I am so glad the weather is cooperating

with us," Mrs. Q. said as everyone unrolled their sleeping bags. "There isn't a cloud in the sky."

"On the last camp-out we got soaked," Marsha told Corrie. "It never stopped raining."

"We even had to have our campfire in the fireplace at the lodge," Jo Ann said. "But it was still fun. We told ghost stories."

"Amy told the best one," Lauren said. "Remember? It was about this guy who marries a woman who always wears a red ribbon around her neck...."

"Oooh...I remember that one!" Jo Ann said. "She won't tell him why. Even though he keeps pestering her. Then years and years later, when she dies, he unties the ribbon. And her head falls off!"

"Gross!" Corrie giggled. "Will we get to tell ghost stories tonight?" she asked Mrs. Q.

"Oh, I bet we will."

"Amy, I hope you know some more real scary ones," Corrie said.

Amy waggled her fingers at Corrie. In her best Count Dracula voice she said, "Maybe. You vill just haff to vait and see." It was a good thing she had brought those monster claws! She wouldn't want to let her friends down.

4

After everybody was unpacked, it was time for lunch. The whole troop gathered around the campsite.

Most of the kids were saying how starved they were. But Amy hardly touched her lunch. The wobbly feeling in her tummy was coming back. Maybe, Amy told herself, it just was because she was so excited to be there. And that was true. She couldn't wait for the real camping stuff to begin.

The first activity was a nature hike through the woods. The troop split into small groups, each with a grown-up leader.

"Now, this isn't any ordinary nature hike," Mrs. Q. told Amy and the other girls in her group. "On this hike we really have to use our eyes. The trick is to look very, very carefully at the things we see along the trail and decide exactly what color they are. And to do that, I brought along these."

Mrs. Q. handed each girl a long strip of paper. Each strip had all different shades of one color, from light to dark. The color sample strips came from the paint store where Mrs. Q.'s husband worked.

"Oh, I get it," Amy said after Mrs. Q. handed her a strip with all different shades of brown. "You mean that I shouldn't just look at a tree or some dirt and say it's brown. I have to look and see what shade of brown it is."

Mrs. Q. nodded. "Exactly."

This sounded like fun. Amy decided to ignore that pesky wobbly feeling in her tummy. It would go away. She turned her baseball cap sideways so the arrow was pointing straight ahead.

"Follow me, troops!" Amy said.

Then off they went.

The hike was fun. Right away Amy started finding interesting matches. A dry leaf was "Camel" brown. An acorn was a color called "Bacon." Under a pine tree Amy found a big umbrella-shaped mushroom. It

matched the brown square on her strip that
was called "Taupe"—whatever that was.

Not too far from the pine tree, Amy
came upon a "Tobacco" brown bird's nest.
Amy's eyes grew wide. The bird's nest was
empty, but it was so round and perfect it
looked like it could have been a drawing in
a picture book.

"Over here!" Amy called out. She was careful not to disturb the nest. "Come look, everybody."

Everyone gathered around Amy's discovery.

"That is soooo cute," said Corrie. "I can just imagine a family of little baby birds living in it."

"Amy, you always find the best stuff," said Jo Ann.

There was even part of a speckled eggshell left in the nest. "I think this nest belonged to some song sparrows," Sarah said, consulting the little field guide that she had brought along with her. "They build their nests on the ground and have freckly eggs."

"What a wonderful find, Amy," Mrs. Q. said. "Thank you for sharing it with us."

Amy smiled. "*De nada*," she said. That was Spanish for "you're welcome." Corrie had taught her how to say it.

Amy looked down at her strip of colors. Now, let's see. She had found something to match every square. All except for "Dark Chocolate." "Dark Chocolate" was a deep, deep brown. Almost black.

Amy knelt down on the ground. Some dirt-colored leaves were very dark brown. But she had already used a leaf for one of her other matches. Amy wanted to find something different. Some nice dark brown bugs, maybe. She peered around some more. But no bugs were in sight.

"Amy!"

Amy looked up. Corrie was motioning to her to catch up with the rest of the group.

Oh wow! Everybody was a lot farther down the trail. They were all sitting on a log, drinking from their water bottles.

"Coming!" Amy called back. She started running toward her friends.

"Amy, remember. No run—" Mrs. Q. never got to finish her sentence.

Amy slipped on some wet leaves. She tried to catch herself. But—thunk—down she went.

Ouch! Amy blinked back tears as everybody came rushing over to her.

"Are you okay?" Mrs. Q. was kneeling beside her.

Amy nodded. She tried to catch her breath. Her knee hurt. Her hand did, too.

"Here, Amy." Corrie patted Amy on the back. "Let me help you up."

Amy winced and shook her head. Not yet.

"And look! Your hat!" Marsha cried. Oh, no! It was all muddy. Her favorite hat!

Amy swallowed hard. She was not—repeat not—going to cry in front of all her friends. She looked down at herself. Her T-shirt and sweatpants were covered with mud. Dark brown, almost black mud.

"Well, I found the last match on my strip." Amy pointed to the "Dark Chocolate" square. "It's chocolate-colored me!"

Everybody giggled. Even Amy.

"Did anybody ever tell you what a good sport you are?" Mrs. Q. asked as she helped Amy to her feet. "Come. We'll get you cleaned up just as soon as we get to the campsite."

A few minutes later Amy was back in the tent, carefully slipping on clean pants over her sore knee.

"That was quite a spill you took," Mrs. Q. said. She cupped Amy's face in her hands. "And remember. You were sick yesterday. Maybe you'd like to stay here in the tent for a little while and just take it easy. I'll keep you company. You probably won't believe this, but I am a world-class slapjack player."

Amy knew Mrs. Q. was trying to be nice. But she shook her head. "No! Please, Mrs. Q.," Amy pleaded, "I don't want to miss out on anything. . . . Besides, what'll the other kids think?"

"The other kids will think that maybe

you need to rest a little." Mrs. Q. was smiling, but her eyes were serious. "You know, these girls are your friends. Sure, everybody thinks you're lots of fun. But they also care about you."

"I know that," Amy said quickly.

"I hope so." Mrs. Q. did not sound entirely convinced.

But, with Amy's promise to tell Mrs. Q. if she wasn't feeling well, they joined the rest of the troop.

5

It was a busy afternoon. The girls learned how to tie lots of different knots. They helped pitch a pup tent. And they went for a canoe ride to the other side of the lake. Once they got there, Mrs. Q. took a picture of each Brownie by the most amazing tree. It was completely hollow and roomy enough for Amy and Corrie to stand inside together.

It was all fun stuff. Exactly the kind of stuff Amy had been looking forward to

doing on the camp-out, and she certainly
tried her hardest to have a good time. But
that was the problem. With her tummy ache
and her knee hurting, it was hard to have a
good time. Having fun seemed more like
work.

At dinner Amy stared at the hot dog she
had just finished cooking over the campfire.
Maybe if she tried to eat she would feel
better. Maybe she was hungry and she didn't
know it.

Corrie was sitting cross-legged next to
her. She sighed happily as she licked mustard
off her fingers. "It's so pretty here in the
woods. I never saw so many stars in the sky.
There must be a zillion."

Amy nodded. She made herself take a few
bites of her hot dog. It tasted like rubber
to her.

"You were right, Amy," Corrie went on.
"Camp-outs are so much fun. I wish we
were staying for two nights. Don't you?"

Amy managed a weak smile. The truth
was she found herself thinking of home.
How nice it would be to take a bubble
bath. And after that she could put on her
favorite nightgown. The one that had blue
lambs printed all over it. Amy pictured her
bed with the flowered quilt. Part of her
wanted to be in that bed right now.

"I hope we get to tell ghost stories soon," Corrie said.

Ghost stories. Oh no! The monster claws. They were still in her duffel bag back at the tent. Amy had forgotten all about them.

Lauren was sitting on the other side of Amy. She heard what Corrie had said.

"That's right! Mrs. Q. Mrs. Q.!" Lauren tugged on Mrs. Q.'s sweatshirt. "Can we tell ghost stories now? Please. You said we could. Remember?"

"Well, it seems like everybody is just about finished eating." Mrs. Q. looked around the circle of girls. "So why not? I could use a good scare myself."

"Yesssss!" Several Brownies punched the air with their fists.

Mrs. Q. went around the campfire circle, starting with one of the younger girls. Any

Brownie who wanted to could tell a ghost story.

"I can't wait to hear yours!" Corrie whispered to Amy.

What should she do? She didn't want to let Corrie and the other kids down. And Amy did have her flashlight with her. She supposed she could ask Mrs. Q. to let her go back to the tent for a minute.

It was Lauren's turn now. That meant Amy was next.

"Long, long ago in a dark, spooky house that was known as Blackwood Hall..." Lauren began.

Amy chewed her lower lip. Everyone would be counting on her for a good story. She really should get the claws. The tent was only a little ways away. Amy could see it from here. The trouble was Amy was afraid to move. Her tummy felt really, really weird. Eating that hot dog had been a big mistake. Uh-oh. Better not—repeat not— even think about hot dogs!

Lauren was finishing up her story now. "...And so the sad ghost of Blackwood Hall could rest in peace. At last."

Uh-oh. Amy's turn now.

Everyone was looking at her. They all had smiles on their faces, like a present was about to be unwrapped and they knew something good was inside.

"Oooh! I'm scared already," Corrie squealed.

Amy swallowed hard. The hot dog in her tummy felt like it was growing bigger and bigger. She did not want to disappoint anybody. But she didn't feel well.

"Ummmmm. I'm sorry, you guys. I don't have any story." Amy kept her eyes on the campfire. "I don't feel so hot. All I really want to do is go to bed."

Mrs. Q. got up quickly. She started toward Amy. "That's perfectly okay, sweetie—"

"Mrs. Q.!" Lauren was giggling. "Amy's just talking opposite talk. She feels fine. She doesn't want to go to bed—she wants to tell a ghost story!"

Some of the girls started giggling.

"Mrs. Q. really fell for that one!" someone else said.

"This is not opposite talk! I'm not kidding. Get it?" Amy's words came out sounding much louder than she meant. And madder.

"I know, sweetie," Mrs. Q. said. "It's okay—"

No, it wasn't!

All of a sudden Amy's tummy rocked so hard it felt like it was turning a cartwheel. Amy tried to swallow hard. But it was no use. She knew what was coming next.

Amy leaned over and threw up.

"Amy!" several voices cried.

"Come, girls. There's no need to get excited," Mrs. Q. said. She was holding Amy's braid back in case she needed to throw up again.

"Oh, Amy!" Corrie said with concern. "I'm so sorry you're sick." She almost sounded as if she was going to cry.

All of a sudden tears welled up in Amy's eyes. Whatever was the opposite of fun, that's what she was having. Amy wished her mother was here. Ma would rub her tummy. Ma would stroke her forehead until she felt better. The tears began to spill down Amy's cheeks. And out came words she never expected to say. "I—I—I want to go home!"

The whole troop grew very quiet.

Mrs. Q. brushed a strand of hair off Amy's face and said very softly, "I'm going to take you over to the lodge now. That's if you feel up to it. I think you will be more comfortable there."

Amy nodded. Without another word she followed Mrs. Q. away from the campfire.

6

In the lodge was a little room with two cots. Amy was in one of them with Mrs. Q. sitting beside her.

"I can stay here with you all night. Krissy S.'s mother will sleep in our tent instead of me. We always bring an extra mom or two along. Just for situations like this." Mrs. Q. patted Amy's hand. "Feeling better?"

Amy nodded. All the rocking and cartwheels in her tummy had stopped. But what a mess she had made...throwing up in front of everybody! "I am so embarrassed. I—"

Mrs. Q. put a finger to her lips. "Shhh. No more about that. You just close your eyes now and rest."

So Amy did. She snuggled down in the cot. The pillow and blankets were so soft. And with Mrs. Q. stroking her forehead, the same way her mother would, Amy fell fast alseep.

In the morning Amy felt much, much better. Well, maybe just one "much" better. She still wanted to stay right where she was. In bed.

The first-aider brought Amy toast and something warm to drink.

"Mrs. Cohen will stay here in the lodge

with you in case you need anything," Mrs. Q. told Amy. "I'll check in later. But I have to go help out with the scavenger hunt now."

The scavenger hunt. Amy was sad to miss it. She thought about all the fun the Brownies were going to have. Without her. Amy pulled the blanket up to her chin.

Well, she sure had made last night a fun time for everyone... throwing up, crying in front of everybody, and carrying on about how she wanted to go home. What would her friends think of her?

Throughout the morning, Amy kept glancing out the window. She hoped Corrie or some of the other kids would stop by to wave and see how she was feeling. But nobody came.

Later on the bell by the flagpole started ringing. That meant it was time for the closing campfire ceremony. Amy was sad to miss that, too.

The closing campfire was not for telling jokes or ghost stories or singing funny songs. It was more serious, but Amy loved it best of anything. Last time the girls took turns reading the story they had written together about Juliette Low. She was the lady who started Girl Scouts in America.

Today the troop was going to sing songs from all over the world. The songs were about friendship. In French. In Spanish. In Swahili. They were beautiful songs that made Amy feel part of something BIG, something important.

Friendship. Amy thought about how everybody was always telling her how popular she was and how many friends she had. But what did "popular" mean anyway? If she wasn't being tons of fun, did kids still like her? It seemed as though nobody even noticed she was gone.

Amy sighed. Maybe she would take a nap. After all, there was nothing else to do. This camp-out sure hadn't turned out like she thought it would.

7

When Mrs. Q. woke her up, it was to tell her that everybody was ready to go home.

"We've got you all packed up. Mrs. Cohen will drive you home in her car." Mrs. Q. handed Amy some fresh clothes. "The last thing you need is a bumpy bus ride."

Amy nodded. Mrs. Q. was right. But she was missing the ride home, too.

"Well, tell everybody good-bye for me."

"Why not tell them yourself?"

"What?"

"Take a look outside." Mrs. Q. smiled.

Amy did.

There was her whole troop!

They were standing in a line holding big cutout letters. All together they spelled out "FEEL BETTER, AMY." There were two girls for every letter. Except the "Y." Corrie held that by herself.

"The girls decided to skip the scavenger hunt this morning. Instead they made the world's biggest get well card for you," Mrs. Q. said. "It was all their idea."

"I can't believe this!" Amy said. She felt that she must look the way cartoon characters did after they got clunked on the head with a lead weight.

Then one by one the girls said what their letter stood for. Lauren and Marsha said that the "F" in FEEL was for "very, very, very and so on very good FRIEND. We really mean it." The "E's" were for

"EXCEPTIONALLY nice in EVERY way."
The "L" was for "making us LAUGH a
lot." "B" was "We're sorry that you
BARFED."

Amy giggled at that one.

On and on it went all the way to Corrie.

"Y," said Corrie. "Y is for YOU. There is nobody else like you in the whole world, and that's why we hope you—"

"FEEL BETTER, AMY!" the troop finished together.

Amy swallowed hard. Her friends had done this just for her. All of a sudden she had a funny feeling in her tummy. Not like she was going to throw up or anything. It was a warm, good feeling.

"Thanks, everybody. Thanks so much!" She really had the best friends ever.

"See you tomorrow at school," the girls called out.

Corrie was the last to go. She waved and blew a kiss. "Bye, buddy!"

Amy watched the troop pile into the big yellow bus.

"I'll call you tonight to see how you're feeling," Mrs. Q. told Amy. Then she gave her a big hug. "I hope you see how special you are to us all...even when you're sick and not being funny."

Amy nodded. She did.

Mrs. Q. headed for the bus. A minute later the big yellow bus pulled up the hill.

Well, Amy had been right. The camp-out had certainly not turned out like she thought. Amy imagined telling her parents how she fell in the mud and wrecked her baseball cap, how she threw up in front of everyone, and how she even had to stay in bed and miss all the stuff today.

As the bus turned onto the dirt road, Amy could hear her friends singing,

"Found a peanut.

Found a peanut..."

Amy smiled. Still, in some way, this camp-out really had been great. And that was not—repeat not—opposite talk!

Girl Scout Ways

Amy and her Brownie troop had lots of fun on their nature hike. What made the hike special was using the color strips. You and your troop can plan a color strip nature hike, too!

- Before you go, you'll need to get color strips from a hardware store. You can ask one of your parents or your troop leader to get them for you. Or, if there's a store in your neighborhood, you can stop in and ask a store clerk for some color strips. Make sure to get colors that you can see often in nature. For example, orange, brown, yellow, and green are all good colors. Get enough color strips for everyone who is going on the hike.

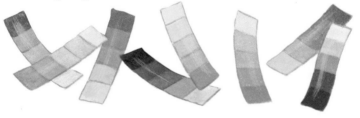

- Ask your troop leader, or another grown-up to come along on the hike. Then choose a park or some woods that are familiar.

- On the hike, try to find at least one thing that matches each color on the strip. At first it might not seem like anything matches, but if you look *really* closely, the colors will begin to stand out. You can find lots of different colors in nature!

- Once everyone has matched the colors, have each girl lead the other girls around to show what she has found. It's important to leave everything exactly as you found it. Some matches will be really special, like Amy's bird's nest. Other things more common, like grass or leaves. You'll be surprised at all the matches you and your friends will find!